The Story of Pink Jade

By William J. Lederer

ALL THE SHIP'S AT SEA

THE LAST CRUISE

SPARE-TIME ARTICLE WRITING FOR MONEY

ENSIGN O'TOOLE AND ME

THE UGLY AMERICAN (with Eugene Burdick)

A NATION OF SHEEP

SARKHAN (with Eugene Burdick)

TIMOTHY'S SONG

The Story

# of Pink Jade

by WILLIAM J. LEDERER

Illustrations by JOAN BERG VICTOR

New York

W · W · NORTON & COMPANY · INC ·

The Story of Pink Jade

It was a long, long time ago,

in the fourth month

of the Year of the Sparrow

Winter was over; and the East Wind had
returned, bringing life to the earth. At the
palace of Pink Jade-the-Beautiful, crocus
buds pushed through the soil toward the
yellow sun; and young bamboos whispered
on the hillsides.

Most of the world rejoiced. Thrushes
sang to one another on the eaves; and
nightingales opened their throats to heaven.
Fish jumped and sparkled in the lake.

But within the palace everything was dark and silent, for winter remained in Pink Jade's heart; and in her mind was fear. She was afraid because there were no more kingly lovers to woo her, to admire her, to bring her gifts.

She said to herself, "If there are no more suitors, how can I be amused?"

For many years, mighty kings, bewitched by Pink Jade's loveliness, had come from distant lands. They tried to win her with rich treasures. Many had offered their kingdoms.

Pink Jade had used each royal lover until she wearied of him or he had no more gifts; and, eventually, each in turn had departed, humiliated and poor.

Now there was no one left worthy of her favor.

Pink Jade said to her servants, "Where is there a mighty sovereign? Somewhere there must be another potentate!"

They touched their heads to the floor, but none spoke. Even the thrushes and the nightingales were silent now.

"I must have an answer," said Pink Jade. "Send for Aga, the wise man."

The servants hurried away to find Aga; and Pink Jade continued walking about her vast halls. Everywhere there were mirrors. She looked at herself; and for a moment was pleased. Her dress of white gossamer silk shimmered like mist passing before a silver moon. About her breasts there hung a dazzling string of emeralds and garnets and tourmaline.

Pink Jade began to dance. She swayed with a panther's grace, each motion showing the curves and softness of her womanhood. With a wild shake of her head, her dance quickened. The fragrance of Pink Jade filled the room like the breath of roses; and her black hair, like cascades of midnight, tumbled to her slender waist. In the passion of her dance she smiled, and the brightness of it seemed to illuminate the chamber as if a thousand lamps had been lighted. It was in this fashion that Pink Jade had enchanted and vanquished the kings who had come to win her.

Suddenly Pink Jade stopped. Some peasant women and their children were passing by the palace. They wore ragged clothes, their hands were red, and their faces were wrinkled from weather and hunger. "They work all day in the fields," thought Pink Jade. "They bear many children and lose their youth and beauty. They have no servants, no wealth. Yet they laugh merrily among themselves and sing when they work. And I who have riches, fame, and servants, I am now dissatisfied and seldom laugh."

Pink Jade did not understand. She only knew that nothing amused her anymore. That very afternoon she had summoned entertainers. There had been an Indian magician who had made an elephant disappear. There had been acrobats who had jumped fifteen feet into the air and turned six somersaults before they landed. There had been quick-eyed jugglers and clowns.

After their performance she had stamped her foot and cried, "They are dull, stupid. Get rid of them all."

Pink Jade watched the peasant women until they were out of sight.

She called for her jewel chest and gazed at the sparkling treasures. The fiery diamonds were the gift of an emperor of Africa. The sapphires which seemed to splash like blue waterfalls were tribute from the Czar of Russia. The rubies—each the size of a red flamingo's egg—were brought by the Shah of Persia. The Shah also had given her a marble jar of wondrous ointment brewed from rare herbs found only in the Elburz Mountains. Pink Jade turned away. Now even her treasures did not give her pleasure.

"Perhaps my beauty is a curse," said Pink Jade. "Once men see me, they wish to be my slaves. My victories are so easy that I am bored. If only I could find a lover who could everlastingly enchant me."

A servant announced, "Aga, the wise man, awaits without."

"Let him enter," said Pink Jade.

Aga came in. He walked with two crooked canes, his back bent by the weight of many winters.

"Oh Aga, wisest man in Cathay," said Pink Jade, "many times I have heard you speak of the king of kings, the emperor of all nations, the lord of all the worlds, the monarch of all universes . . ."

The wise man nodded.

Pink Jade smiled. "Aga, summon the king of kings here. It will please me to dance before him and perhaps he can amuse me."

Aga pressed his pale lips together and hung his head in silence.

"Did you hear my command?"

He stared into Pink Jade's eyes and said, "No mortal can summon the king of kings. If you were to send all your soldiers to bring him to you, they would fail. No, if you wish to dance before the king of kings, then you must go to him. But first you must find him."

"Where is he?"

"It is said he is everywhere. But the chronicles state that his ruby throne is on the peak of the Tallest Mountain."

"Aga," said Pink Jade, "you will direct me to the Tallest Mountain."

He frowned. "It is said that only holy men and saints have been known to find the lord."

Pink Jade spoke impatiently. "Aga, you will take me to the Tallest Mountain."

"I am too old," said Aga, "but I will draw you a map. The way is in the direction where the sun sets at this time of year. Thirty moons away it is. Between here and the Tallest Mountain, where it is said the Lord sits, are deserts, swamps, lands of ice and snow, terrible jungles, and the Tumultuous River. It is an almost impossible journey."

"I will find this god and dance before him," said Pink Jade. "When he sees my beauty, he will surely amuse me more than the lesser kings. You will be on the Tallest Mountain with me and you will see for yourself."

Aga did not reply.

Pink Jade summoned her chief slave. She told him to prepare for the journey and warned, "Many strong backs will be needed to carry a god's throne back to my palace."

On the tenth day of the Month

of the Warm Winds, Pink Jade-the-Beautiful stepped into her new palanquin. It was
a present from the Emperor of Cathay and
it blazed with powdered gold and sapphires.
From its azure silk canopy a heaven of silver moons and stars shimmered, making a
gentle twilight of their own.

"Let the journey begin," said Pink Jade.

The chief slave cracked a long whip, the
palanquin was lifted, and Pink Jade's caravan moved westward on the twelve thousand li trip to the Tallest Mountain.

Ahead ran dwarfs in red and yellow garments which tinkled with small bells. Bobbing grotesque heads from side to side, the dwarfs pranced along on crooked legs, turning somersaults and crying out in high-pitched voices, "Make way! Make way for the Princess of Beauty! She is going forth to conquer the lord!"

Behind the dwarfs danced slender youths in pointed shoes of purple alligator leather, pirouetting as they tossed jasmine blossoms before the palanquin. At a distance of one li before the caravan strode six giants dressed in iron jerkins. They smote brass cymbals so large that their clang could be heard as far away as the eye could see.

On all sides marched broad-backed slaves and soldiers carrying spears and bows. And then came camels, plodding along silently under heavy loads. On one of the camels rode Aga, the wise man.

The dwarfs took up the cry again. "Make way! Make way! The Princess of Beauty is coming! She is going forth to conquer the lord."

A blue jay jumped from the lowest branches of a small tree and chattered back, "Beautiful but wicked! Beautiful but wicked!"

The soldiers loosed their arrows at the bird, but the jay flew away unscathed, still chattering, "Beautiful but wicked! Beautiful but wicked!"

The caravan moved through the country where men grow barley and then through the land of rice paddies; and then over the red mountains where it was said escaped criminals lived in caves.

After ten full moons had shone and faded, the caravan reached the edge of the desert. Strewn on the glaring sands were white skeletons of other travelers who had attempted the crossing.

The caravan moved more slowly now. Aga led the way. The old, wrinkled man seldom spoke. He breathed slowly and shallowly, so that the heat would not sear his lungs.

It became hotter and hotter. The sun seemed to be a sheet of flame. Men began to weaken. Casks of water ran low. Within a moon and a half, the dwarfs and the slender youths died from heat and thirst: But Pink Jade was comfortable. Within her shaded palanquin, slaves bathed her often in precious water. She looked into her mirror and fancied what the king of kings would do after he had seen her incomparable loveliness.

In the Month of the Willow Tree, the caravan—much smaller now—reached the end of the desert. In front of them they saw a great swamp. Clouds of gnats swarmed over it. Steam hissed from hidden pools.

After but two days of rest, Pink Jade ordered the caravan to move through the swamp. Marsh grass was so tall and thick that one person could not see another if he were but three paces away. Underfoot was mud that often turned to quicksand. From above, flesh-eating vultures swooped down, screeching, looking for carrion.

Pink Jade drew the curtains of her palanquin and stayed within, night and day.

The slaves, clumsy with heavy loads, sank into the mire and quicksand. The camels floundered. Those who managed to find paths of firm ground still were not safe. They had to fight off poisonous insects and orange-colored lizards whose teeth were like needles.

Within a moon the slaves and camels were gone, and soldiers had to take turns carrying Pink Jade's palanquin. Even Aga's camel had been lost. Now the old man walked. Leaning on two soldiers, he moved awkwardly through the mud.

Every evening, Pink Jade summoned him and asked, "Aga, how long will it be before I find the king of kings?"

Aga always answered her the same way. "In the Month of the Harvest, if you are still alive, Pink Jade, you will reach the Tallest Mountain."

"But what about the king of kings?"

"I can but lead you to the mountain."

When the caravan emerged from the swamp, only Pink Jade, Aga, the chief slave, and the strongest of the soldiers were still alive. And ahead of them was the land of eternal winter.

When they reached it, they could see only ice and snow; and hear only the wind. There was no way for members of the caravan to warm themselves. The small supply of wood was used for the brazier in Pink Jade's palanquin. The men's teeth chattered and their limbs froze. The armor which the soldiers wore became as cold as the ice itself. Although the soldiers were strong and brave, they could not fight off the wind; and when the cold reached their bones, Pink Jade's warriors fell into the deep snow.

After a moon of trudging in the land of eternal winter, Pink Jade marveled that Aga still survived, twisted and bent, leaning into the wind that tore at his ragged clothing. She asked herself, "Is there not some way to keep him warm?"

He must be kept alive. She had a need of him.

Wrapping fur garments about herself, Pink Jade stepped from her comfortable palanquin; and she bade Aga to enter, ride in it, and warm himself.

"And you, beautiful lady," asked Aga. "What will you do?"

35   "I will walk for a while."

"Every hour you share your palanquin," said Aga, "brings you a thousand li nearer to the king of kings."

"I do not understand," said Pink Jade.

"Perhaps you will one day," he said.

Pink Jade smiled as she trudged through the snow. "Aga is getting very old and the journey has weakened his mind," she thought.

But, from then on, whenever she walked in the cold while Aga rode in her palanquin, Pink Jade thought about Aga's words.

She noticed that the few soldiers still alive also were freezing; and during those times when she was in the warm palanquin, she lent her furs to them. After all, it was to her advantage to keep them alive.

This gave her a pleasure she had not experienced before; and she wondered about it. Yet while she wondered, the vicious cold wind increased, blowing out the lives of one or two each day.

On one freezing sunrise, Pink Jade found Aga lying in the snow, stiff and blue. She tried to revive him by feeding him her own precious hot tea. But even as he drank it, the life ebbed from him. Aga weakly tapped Pink Jade's gold teacup with his fingers and said, "Pink Jade, this teacup is the way to god."

37 And then he died.

Once more Pink Jade did not understand.

She re-entered the warm palanquin and ordered her caravan forward. Now there were only six people alive.

Finally the land of eternal winter came to an end, and in front of Pink Jade was the jungle.

At the edge of the dark morass, Pink Jade stepped out of her palanquin. Four soldiers, the last of her guard, lay on the ground; they were too weak to go on.

Pink Jade pointed to the west and said to her chief slave, "On the other side of the jungle is the Tallest Mountain. I am almost there!"

He replied, "Oh, beautiful mistress, many many moons have come and gone. There is no one left to carry your palanquin."

"We will continue," said Pink Jade.

The two of them pushed into the tangle of vines and trees. The slave coughed frequently and tired easily, but he moved ahead, cutting a path with his long scimitar. Even so, the thorns and rough-barked vines scratched Pink Jade's skin and tore her clothing. But this did not worry her. She often smiled as she patted the small bundle she carried. It contained the silk gossamer dress which she always had worn when she danced before kingly suitors, and it also contained the marble jar of precious beauty ointment.

39

Three moons later, in the Month of the Harvest and in the Year of the Fox, Pink Jade and her slave reached the other side of the jungle.

The slave pointed and shouted, "Oh, mistress, there it is!"

Thirty li away, the Tallest Mountain towered into the sky. The bottom was black rock. The upper half dazzled with ice and snow. At the top it glowed ruby red.

"Ah, the throne of the king of kings," said Pink Jade. "And there, protecting the mountain is the Tumultuous River." she looked about. A frown darkened her face. "I will need a raft; and there are no trees near the river. I am so close, but without a raft I cannot reach the ruby throne."

"I will cut tree trunks from the jungle," said the slave, "and drag them to the riverside, and I will make ropes from vines and build for you, Beautiful One, a raft to cross the river. I will collect nuts and dry berries and other food to last you for several moons, and then I will ferry you across the river and help you up the Tallest Mountain.

Pink Jade put her hand on the shoulder of her slave, saying, "You have pleased me. All the others, the hundreds of slaves and servants and soldiers died during the journey. Even Aga deserted me. Only you have been true and I wish to reward you. I hereby free you. You are no longer a slave. You are now my servant. And soon, when I am Queen of the Universe, you shall have a palace of your own, and slaves and riches."

His face was radiant. Dropping to his knees, he bowed his head.

Pink Jade knew she never could find another slave as devoted as this one. Deep inside, she felt a small ache, as if she had lost or given away something precious. The loss made her suffer, yet it was a pain which did not hurt.

She said, "It is getting dark. We will rest now. In the morning we will need all our strength."

At sunrise, the peak of the Tallest Mountain again glowed red. "Soon I will be at the mightiest monarch's throne," thought Pink Jade. "We must hurry."

For two moons the servant hauled logs thirty li from the jungle, over jagged rocks, to the edge of the river. He made a raft and collected food. He helped Pink Jade gather herbs to heal her scratches and cuts. She did not use her precious ointment because she was saving it. The ointment brought strength and youth and beauty; and she would anoint herself just before she danced.

Finally, at the river's edge, the servant completed the raft. But the river was so broad and swift that the raft had to be taken far upstream so that they could cross without being swept over great falls and smashed on the rocks below.

It was difficult for one man to pull the heavy raft quickly. Pink Jade became impatient. Standing close to her perspiring servant, she grasped the line and helped him. Now the raft moved upstream more speedily.

At the end of the day, Pink Jade looked at the rope splinters in her hands and the raw patches on her shoulders. "Oh," she thought, "and to think that not long ago I had over a hundred slaves."

When they were far enough up river, the two of them embarked on the raft. The river swept them downstream, but the servant had fashioned a broad oar, and with it he paddled furiously. When they reached the other side, he was exhausted and coughing; but Pink Jade insisted they immediately start up the mountain.

The jagged black rock cut their sandals. The snowy peak seemed to be an impossible distance in the sky. But its top glowed red. Pink Jade smiled and clasped her bundle containing her silk dress and beauty ointment.

Day after day they climbed. Always the path became steeper and the air colder. The servant coughed more and more. His breath came with difficulty; and during the night he trembled with fever. On the fifth morning he tried to get up, but was too weak.

"Leave me here, mistress," he said, "I am dying and am but a burden."

Pink Jade looked up at the glowing mountain top. For a moment she grew angry at the man's helplessness and thought of whipping him. When she came close, she saw that he was smiling and not afraid. She heard him say, "Do not worry, mistress. Everyone who truly seeks god will find him. For some it is harder than for others."

She did not understand, but her anger left. She thought, "After all, I have been seeking the king of kings for years now. Another day's delay cannot matter."

So Pink Jade nursed her servant. She gave him herbs and food. She massaged him and wrapped him in her silk coat and lay close to keep him warm. She thought, "All my life I have beguiled men with my beauty and dancing. It was easy, and it bored me. Now I am trying to heal my servant from whom I will receive neither gifts nor amusement. It is hard, and yet I am not bored."

After two days, he had not improved. He grew paler and weaker. Pink Jade was certain she knew how to arouse him. As if preparing for an emperor, she put on her famous gossamer dress. She danced and sang before her servant, but he did not get well. She even bent and caressed him, but he lay still.

The thought of failure frightened her. She opened her precious bundle and took out her beauty salve. She anointed the man, and life immediately flowed into him again. Suddenly young and vigorous, he stood up, flexed his muscles, and began leading her up the mountain.

Once more the strange feeling was strong within Pink Jade's chest. She knew she had given away half her precious, irreplaceable ointment, yet she felt joy.

The next morning when she called to him, her servant did not get up. He was an old man again, wrinkled, pale, and with the pallor of death upon him. His eyes barely opened and his lips quavered. "Oh, my mistress, your magic ointment made me young last night. I bless you for your generosity.

But the lotion does not last. It turns quickly into mist, and when it disappears life and strength go with it."

He closed his eyes, and Pink Jade knew he was dead. There was no fear on his face, only a smile. It was a happy, serene smile, far different than that which she had seen on the faces of her many lovers.

She felt a few drops of warm rain sliding down her cheeks. "I have never known rain to be warm," she said, "and there are no clouds in the sky. How strange." The drops reached her mouth and they were salty.

The strange feeling was stronger now.

Far above, the top of the mountain glowed more brightly than ever. Pink Jade shook her tiny fist at it and shouted, "I'll be there soon to dance for you, oh lord." Alone now, she began climbing as fast as she could.

Several days later, she looked down into the valley far below. She saw a black speck moving from the distant jungle across the rocks to the Tumultuous River. It was a man. By evening he was at the edge of the river; and Pink Jade saw him walking up and down the bank.

"I wonder," Pink Jade thought, "who he is?"

She became uneasy. "What is a stranger doing here?" she thought. "Could it be that he, too, is seeking god and the precious ruby throne?"

The thought angered her; and, in temper, she kicked a huge round rock. It tumbled down the side of the mountain. She watched it smash down the steep sides. It kept going down, down, down, moving ever more rapidly, and finally it splashed into the river close to where her raft was tied.

Then she wondered if the stranger could be a holy man? Aga had said that only holy men or saints could find the lord and look upon him.

She continued climbing; but after a few minutes she found herself again watching the stranger. It was clear now that he wanted to come to the mountain. Several times he tried to swim across the river, but each time he was swept downstream and had to return to the far bank.

Pink Jade thought, "If he is a holy man, perhaps he might make my search a little easier."

She watched as he attempted, again and again, to swim across the river, each time failing; and Pink Jade realized that he could not cross without a raft.

"If I go down and help him," she thought, "he will get here more quickly than if I just wait and watch."

She started down. It was a long way and she reached the bottom just before dark.

She remembered that her raft must be moved upstream before it was possible to cross the river. The next morning she put the halter of rope around her shoulders and began pulling the raft. Slowly she moved the raft, resting often.

Finally she was far enough upstream. She climbed on the raft and pushed into the swirling river. It careened downstream, but Pink Jade paddled hard and reached the other side. When she at last pushed the raft ashore, the man ran toward her. He embraced her.

"You were halfway to the top," he said, "yet you came back to help me on my pilgrimage so that I, too, could look upon the lord and be blessed."

Pink Jade felt the warm rain on her cheeks again.

She was tired, but she was anxious to reach the top of the mountain. Pink Jade and the pilgrim pulled the heavy raft upstream and paddled to the other side.

For the next six days they climbed rapidly. On the seventh morning the pilgrim fell where the incline was steep. The rock was slippery, and the man slid downward. There was nothing for him to clutch onto. He could not stop, and Pink Jade saw him disappear into a deep crevice. When she reached him, the man was bleeding badly. As she bent over to examine him, dark clouds covered the sky, and great sounds of thunder came from the top of the mountain.

"My dear friend," said the pilgrim, "we must accept god's will. I am dying. Leave me here and go up the mountain alone. Do you hear the thunder? It is god's voice. He is calling."

Pink Jade heard it. She thought, "This holy man understands the language of god. He can be of much help to me."

Once more she opened her precious bundle. She bandaged the pilgrim's wounded chest with her silk gossamer dress. She anointed the man with some of her precious ointment.

Youth and life returned to the pilgrim immediately, but soon he grew weak again, and died. Pink Jade was puzzled by the serene and joyful look upon his face.

She thought, "I used my gossamer silk gown to stop his bleeding, and I anointed him with my beauty potion, but still he died."

The thunder continued and Pink Jade wondered what the king of kings was saying. Was he mocking her or pleading with her to make haste?

She continued climbing, slowly now because of the steepness. Once when she paused to rest she saw several more black specks far below on the other side of the river.

"Oh, no," said Pink Jade, "I will not go down again and help them. I am almost all the way to the throne. Let them cross the river as best they can. Let them build a raft as I did so many, many moons ago. I am almost at the top now."

She recalled how difficult her trip had been—how she had started endless moons ago, with her huge caravan and with many slaves; and how soldiers had cleared people from the path of her palanquin, and how the dwarfs had shouted, "Make way for the Princess of Beauty! She is going forth to conquer the lord!"

Now her caravan was gone, the soldiers, slaves, and animals all dead. She was alone. Her gossamer dress was ruined and bloody. She had nothing left except a tiny portion of her magic ointment. Ice cut her feet and cold winds from the summit slashed her. Her breath came hard and her body ached. Up and up she struggled. Yet with every hour she moved closer to the summit. The thunder never ceased.

She was so high now that she could see the other peaks beyond. Then she made a discovery. *It was from the other peaks that the thunder was coming.* Pink Jade saw that the other mountains seemed to be moving, and she knew that their motion made the thunder.

Now she understood the roar. The glaciers of ice and snow which lay just beyond the Tallest Mountain were cracking and moving down into the valley of the Tumultuous River. Within a few days the immeasurable masses of ice and snow would slide down into the flat areas where the newly arrived strangers waited. To escape, they must either cross the river and climb the mountain or flee back into the jungle.

But the people could not know they were in danger. From where they were, across the river, the thundering, descending glaciers were not visible.

Pink Jade stared at the tiny black specks. "No!" she shouted above the winds. "No! I cannot go down to help them. I am almost at the throne, and I must go on."

She turned and started climbing again. The way was harder now than it had been. The sides were steep and slippery; and Pink Jade had to feel her way, one step at a time, testing each foothold, holding on to jagged ice outcroppings with her hands. Yet she struggled upward, often crying out, "I am coming, oh god, I am coming to dance for you."

At night blizzards howled and froze her; and during the day the sun was so close that Pink Jade's skin blistered, even though she was chattering from cold. Yet with every hour she moved a little nearer to the summit.

At sunrise on the twenty-fifth day of the Midwinter Month, Pink Jade was so weak she could hardly move. She crawled to the top of a steep ridge and, suddenly, there in front of her was the peak of the Tallest Mountain. It glowed a deep red.

"At last, at last I am here."

She looked about, but saw no throne. There was nothing but a pinnacle of ice, and it was the sun which made it red.

Pink Jade shouted, "God, I have come to dance for you."

There was no answer except the roaring of the wind and the thunder of the avalanches sliding from the nearby mountains.

For a moment Pink Jade stood still, shivering and silent. Then her muscles collapsed and her joints seemed to explode and melt. She shuddered; and, as if possessed by a demon, ran crazily about the jagged pinnacle shouting, "Lord! Lord!" She flung herself into icy caves, scratching frantically at icy walls, calling loudly, "Lord, where are you?" Like a wild animal she got on her hands and knees and peered into crevices; and she burrowed into deep snowdrifts.

But she found nothing.

Pink Jade fell, exhausted. Raising herself upon her elbows, she stared into the ice— and then she screamed. A fearful witch grimaced back at her. It was a reflection of herself. The years of travel and hardship had stolen her youth and beauty. Pink Jade was an old woman now, a frightened hag with white coarse hair, cracked skin, and a wrinkled face with tight, rough lips.

She wept; and now, for the first time, she knew the warm raindrops that tasted like salt came from within her.

"I have lost everything," she thought, "searching for this god—my beauty, my wealth, my very life. I have given up everything for *this*," she said, looking at the pinnacle of ice. "And now I haven't even the strength to go back."

She wept again; and she recalled the other times when tears had flown from her. It was when she had nursed her servant; and once more, when she had tried to help the dying pilgrim.

"Those were moments of joy," she thought. She raised her head in astonishment.

Pink Jade's hands and feet were turning blue, her teeth chattered, and she trembled all over.

She heard the thunder and far below on the other side of the river she saw the tiny specks of people. "If they do not flee quickly they will die, just as my servant died and the pilgrim died. The avalanches are moving swiftly toward them."

She gazed at the distant figures far below her and felt a compassion for them she had never had for her kingly lovers. Falling back onto the ice, she moaned, "I would help these people, warn them, if I could. But I am dying, and it is too late."

She flung her arms out, and her hand smashed against the marble ointment jar, breaking it. "There is the very last of me," thought Pink Jade; and immediately she knew what she must do.

With stiff, numb fingers she scraped the few frozen crystals of ointment from the broken marble. There was only a palmful— and Pink Jade rubbed the hard crystals into her skin. Soon she was warmer and she felt the strength of youth surge through her.

She started down the mountain, running, sliding, falling—hurrying desperately because the effect of the ointment would not last long; and when it was gone, Pink Jade would die. Down, down, she went, careening, leaping crevices, often falling. Her feet bled, her lungs seemed to be filled with fire, but she kept on.

By the time she reached the river, the strength from the ointment had vanished, and Pink Jade fell to the ground, now unable to move.

On the other side of the river, the people waved. Pink Jade, forced herself to crawl to the raft; she untied it and put the line about her shoulders. Staggering to her feet, she slowly pulled the raft upstream. How long it took, she did not know. She felt weaker with each faltering step. She drove herself ahead with the thought, "I must warn those people before I die." The roar of the avalanches seemed only a few li away now; but even though Pink Jade wanted to hurry, she could not.

When she arrived at the place where she could start across the river, her swollen hands could hardly hold the crude oar. Even so, she pushed the raft far out into the water and paddled as best she could. Her eyes were misty as if covered by a film; and although the sun was bright, gradually everything became dim. In the semi-darkness she saw the other side of the river draw closer. She reached out and touched the bundle which once had been so precious to her, though now it was worthless. All it contained was a blood-stained dancing gown.

The raft scraped ashore. In a blur, Pink Jade saw the people clustered about her. She tried to speak, but only a thin whisper came out. "Go home!" she murmured. "Go back quickly. The avalanches are coming. Go back or you will die!"

It was almost completely dark now. The thunder from the mountain roared louder than ever. Pink Jade's breath rattled hoarsely in her throat. The people came closer, almost pressing their faces against her. She recognized some of them. Why, there was her slave whom she had freed. Next to him was Aga. And there was the pilgrim she had ferried across the river. Standing beside him were her soldiers, still clad in the furs she had given them.

Her servant smiled. "Ah, how wondrous! She has come at last."

Aga hobbled up and said, "It is our Pink Jade. How beautiful she is!"

The people seemed to fade. The thunder stopped. The darkness fell away. And from the quietness she heard a gentle voice.

"Pink Jade, have you been looking for me?"

How The Story of Pink Jade came to be

In 1940-41, I was a junior officer in the U.S. Navy, and I was attached to the U.S.S. *Tutuila*, a small gunboat moored in the Yangtze River at Chungking, midway between the Himalayas and the China Sea.

On Christmas Day, 1940, I walked to the Second Range—a string of small mountains about ten miles west of Chungking. Near the top of the Second Range I saw several Chinese clustered about a tombstone in an old cemetery. They were burning make-believe money (a favorite offering at the funerals of loved ones), tossing rice about the tombstone, and scattering fragrant dried tangerine peels (the poor man's perfume in Szechuan Province). The people were going through the ritual of paying homage to whomever was buried there.

When the Chinese had left, I inspected the tombstone. It was ancient, but the Chinese characters carved in the hard Szechuan granite still were discernible. I copied them and took them to my friend and teacher, Professor Sing Ho-lin of the Szechuan Institute of Oriental Religion and Philosophy. He translated the characters as follows:

The great Tao created man frail and imperfect. Because of this, man can enjoy the struggle toward perfection. Man is like the seed of the lotus blossom which is buried in the mud. The lotus sprout must push its way through the mud before it can blossom in the sun.

Pink Jade-the-Beautiful lies buried here. It is from her—whose memory we honor—that we have learned of the glory of being frail and imperfect.

That was what was carved on the tombstone. Professor Sing Ho-lin told me that
Pink Jade, for whom the tomb was en-
scribed, had been the most beautiful woman
and the most famous courtesan in China;
and she had lived in the eighth century.
Professor Sing said that almost every Chinese knew the Pink Jade legend; and that
it had been passed from generation to generation by word of mouth.

In April of 1941 the big bombings started, and I forgot about Pink Jade. However,
two years later, about eight thousand miles
away, I heard a very similar tale in Dakar,
Africa. It did not concern a Chinese woman,
of course. Rather, it was about the daughter
of a Negro tribal chief.

In 1949 at the Breadloaf Writers' Con-
ference, at Middlebury College in Vermont,
I heard the legend again. This time it was
told by William Sloane, the author, editor,

and publisher. In his version, the heroine was an American Indian girl who lived near the Rocky Mountains.

I asked Bill where he had learned of the story. He had not read it, he said. He had heard the story from some Navajo Indians.

In 1953 I was in an Igorot settlement near Aparri in the northern Philippines. The villagers had a ritual in which with song and dance, they acted out the same story. This time, it was an Igorot maiden who was the heroine.

By now I knew that the legend of Pink Jade was a universal tale. It is one of those ageless myths which grow spontaneously in communities all over the world, the way trees and flowers grow.

I wanted very much to put the legend on paper; and I have been trying to do so for thirteen years. At first I tried to condense the Chinese, American, African, and Filipino legends all into one, universal version. But it wouldn't work that way; and so, finally, I have written it the way I originally heard it in Chungking, China.

For me, who, like all other human beings, is somewhat frail, and very, very, imperfect, the legend of Pink Jade is a source of comfort and strength. The story illustrates a saying of St. Augustine which goes approximately, "Christianity existed a long time before there was a Jesus; and it lives in some form among all people, even if they have not heard of our Lord by the same name as we have."